GALAXY ZACK

RETURN TO EARTH!

By Ray O'Ryan

Illustrated by Jason Kraft

LITTLE SIMON
New York   London   Toronto   Sydney   New Delhi

LITTLE SIMON
An imprint of Simon & Schuster Children's Publishing Division
1230 Avenue of the Americas, New York, New York 10020
First Little Simon hardcover edition March 2015
Copyright © 2015 by Simon & Schuster, Inc.
Also available in a Little Simon paperback edition.
All rights reserved, including the right of reproduction in whole or in part in any form.
LITTLE SIMON is a registered trademark of Simon & Schuster, Inc., and associated colophon is a trademark of Simon & Schuster, Inc.
For information about special discounts for bulk purchases, please contact Simon & Schuster Special Sales at 1-866-506-1949 or business@simonandschuster.com.
The Simon & Schuster Speakers Bureau can bring authors to your live event. For more information or to book an event contact the Simon & Schuster Speakers Bureau at 1-866-248-3049 or visit our website at www.simonspeakers.com.
Manufactured in the United States of America 0215 FFG
1 2 3 4 5 6 7 8 9 10
Library of Congress Cataloging-in-Publication Data
O'Ryan, Ray.
Return to Earth! / by Ray O'Ryan ; illustrated by Jason Kraft. — First edition.
pages cm. — (Galaxy Zack ; #10)
Summary: "Zack is headed back to Earth for the first time since moving to Nebulon. He can't wait to see Bert and show his new friend, the former bully Seth Stevens, all around his old stomping grounds. When Zack's dog, Luna, escapes and goes missing, sightseeing plans take an unexpected turn. Will Zack find Luna before he has to head home to Nebulon?"
—Provided by publisher.
ISBN 978-1-4814-2181-2 (pbk : alk. paper) — ISBN 978-1-4814-2182-9 (hc : alk. paper) — ISBN 978-1-4814-2183-6 (ebook)
[1. Science fiction. 2. Home—Fiction. 3. Friendship—Fiction.] I. Kraft, Jason, illustrator. II. Title.
PZ7.O7843Re 2015
[Fic]—dc23
2014003843

CONTENTS

Chapter 1
Mystery Planet

Zack Nelson sat at the kitchen table. He was in his house on the planet Nebulon. His dog, Luna, curled up on the floor beside him.

A holographic, 3-D image of stars in space floated above the table.

"This planet-collector that dad just

brought home from Nebulonics is so grape!" said Zack. He ran his finger along the screen of a small handheld device.

Luna tilted her head and yawned. Then she scratched her ear with her back paw.

"It's a game that lets me keep track of every planet I've ever been to. When it shows me a planet I've visited, I have to place it where it belongs in space."

The 3-D image of a small blue planet appeared among the stars.

"That is Araxie," said Zack. "It belongs over here."

Using his finger, Zack moved the floating planet to

a far corner of the star field. Then he tapped on the device again.

A planet covered with orange specks appeared.

"That's Cisnos," Zack said. He moved the planet to where it belonged among the stars. "It has orange mountains."

"Arrrrr," moaned Luna, stretching her front legs.

"I know. Weird, right?"
Zack added a few more planets he had visited since he and his family moved from Earth to Nebulon.

The door to the kitchen elevator slid open. In walked Otto Nelson, Zack's dad. He was home from his job at Nebulonics.

"Hey, Captain, that looks great!" said Dad. He looked up at the planets orbiting above the kitchen table.

Luna jumped up and ran over to greet him.

"Those are all the planets I've been to," Zack said proudly.

"I think you're missing one," said Dad, "and it's an important one. Nebulonics is actually sending me on a business trip to that same special

planet. I think you'd really enjoy coming along. My boss, Fred Stevens, is
going. He's bringing his son, Seth. We
thought maybe you could keep Seth
company and show him around."

When Zack had first arrived on Nebulon, he and Seth got off to a rough start. Although Seth could still be a bit tough to get along with sometimes, the two had since become friends.

"So, it's a planet I've been to?" Zack asked.

"Yup," said Dad.

"Juno? Plexus? Gluco?" guessed Zack. He looked up at all the holographic planets floating above the table.

"Nope," said Dad. A big smile spread across his face. "It's a planet called . . . Earth!"

Chapter 2
Get Ready

In his room, Zack pulled out his über-space duffel bag. He needed to pack fast: They were leaving right after school tomorrow! He began throwing clothes, gadgets, and other stuff into the bag. Each thing he put in was instantly shrunk to a tiny size. This let him fit lots of things inside. When the items were taken out of the bag later, they would return to their original size.

"I can't wait to see the Dubbsville Nine play an actual baseball game," said Zack. He tossed his Dubbsville Nine baseball cap into the bag. It shrunk and vanished inside. "Galactic blast is fun and all, but I miss going to real baseball games."

"Arrrufff!"
Luna barked
in agreement.

"Maybe Bert
can come with
me, just like old
times," said Zack.
"Bert! Holy rondo
bird! I've got to tell
Bert!"

Zack snatched his hyperphone
back out of his bag. He plugged it into
his 3-D holocam and called. Within
seconds, a life-size 3-D image of Bert
appeared in his room.

"Hey, Bert," said Zack. "Guess what! I'm coming to visit Earth tomorrow!"

"Yippie wah-wah!" cried Bert. "That is what you say on Nebulon, right?"

"Yup! Yippie wah-wah!"

"Can't wait to see you!" said Bert.

"We'll be stay-ing with Grams and Gramps," said Zack. "Why don't you meet me there?"

"Great! See you tomorrow night!"

The vid-chat ended. Luna jumped onto Zack's bed and started barking.

"Oh, don't worry, girl," said Zack. "You can come too. I'm sure Dad wouldn't want you to miss out on this trip!"

The next day at school, Zack couldn't think of anything but his trip to Earth. At recess, he ran into Seth Stevens.

"I can't wait to show you all the grape stuff on Earth," said Zack.

"There is nothing you can show me there that I cannot see here," Seth said. "Earth is *way* behind Nebulon on tech and gadgets and robots."

"Yeah, but wait until you taste the pizza on Earth," Zack said. He was trying to get Seth excited about the trip. "You know, pizza was invented on Earth."

"You think it is better than what Ira can make?" Seth asked. "No way!"

Maybe this trip isn't going to be as much fun as I think. Zack worried.

"And, besides, Earthlings are wimpy," Seth said. "I mean, I guess you are okay. But you have been

living on Nebulon for a while."

"So why do you even want to go?" Zack finally asked.

"Are you kidding?" said Seth. "I get to miss a whole day of school!"

Zack sighed. *At least I'll have Luna there to keep me company.*

Chapter 3
Earth!

School finally ended. Zack's Dad and his boss, Fred Stevens, were waiting outside the building.

"You boys ready to visit Earth?" asked Mr. Stevens when Zack and Seth arrived.

"You bet!" cried Zack. He slipped

into the backseat of his dad's flying car. He sat right next to Luna. She happily licked Zack's face.

"Whatever," moaned Seth. He joined Zack in the back.

The car zoomed off into the sky. A few minutes later it arrived at the Creston City Spaceport.

Everyone boarded the shuttle for Earth. Zack hurried to get a window seat.

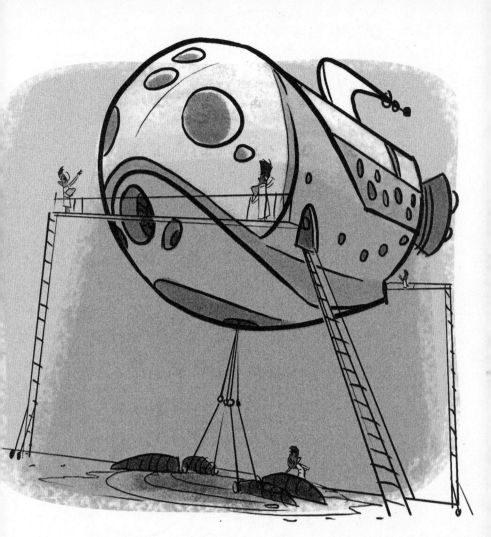

"I want to be the first one to spot
Earth," he said.

The shuttle took off and rocketed into space. Zack remembered that the trip would last a few hours.

"I brought 3-D Cosmic Chess for us to play," said Zack.

Seth shrugged his shoulders and turned toward Zack. "Okay," he said.

Zack pulled a small square vid-screen from his backpack. He pressed a button on the bottom.

A 3-D chessboard sprang from the screen. The chess pieces looked like tiny robots, spaceships, and asteroids.

As the boys took their turns, the pieces on the board acted out each move. Spaceships chased one another around the board. Robots battled, trying to stay out of the way of flying asteroids.

The hours slipped by. Then a tiny blue-and-white dot appeared in the blackness outside the window.

"There it is!" Zack shouted. "Earth!"

He hit the save button so they could continue their game on the trip home.

Earth grew bigger and bigger in the window.

Soon the shuttle landed at the Dubbsville Intergalactic Spaceport.

"Yippee wah-wah!" shouted Zack.

He rushed down the shuttle's ramp. "Back on Earth!"

Seth followed. He stretched his arms and yawned. "Traveling makes me hungry," he complained. "Tell me again what you have to eat on this crazy planet."

Before Zack could answer, Luna

dashed past them and into the
crowded terminal. She sniffed the air
and barked happily.

"Whoa, easy, girl!" cried Zack. He
pulled her leash from his backpack.
"I know you're excited to be back on
Earth, but let's get your leash on."

Before Zack could attach her leash, Luna took off. She raced into the busy spaceport.

"Luna, come back here!" Zack shouted. He and Seth ran after Luna.

But she had already disappeared into the crowd.

Chapter 4

Grams and Gramps

Luna charged into a large crowd of Earthlings and visitors from other planets. She quickly leaped over a small purple Argonian child and headed for the terminal's main entrance.

Seth hurried around the edge of the crowd. He was waiting when

Luna popped out. He scooped her up into his arms. "Where do you think you are going, Luna?" he asked. Zack and the dads caught up.

Zack snapped the leash onto Luna's collar. "That was close." He sighed.

What could have gotten into her? Zack wondered.

"Thanks for catching her, Seth!" Zack said.

Next, they rented a car. They put
their bags into the trunk, and everyone piled in. The bright blue oval lifted
about a foot off the ground. It zoomed
from the spaceport and headed
toward Zack's hometown.

"When do we fly up above the city?" asked Seth.

"Oh, Earth cars don't fly yet, Seth," explained Mr. Nelson. "They hover."

"You guys really are old-fashioned," groaned Seth.

Zack laughed. "But these are brand new! When I left Earth, everyone still had cars with *wheels*."

Seth was shocked.

Soon the hover car arrived at Zack's grandparents' house. Grandma Sonia

and Grandpa Henry rushed over to greet them.

Zack jumped from the car and gave his grandparents big hugs.

"We've missed you so much, Zack," said Grandma Sonia.

"Me too, Grams," said Zack, smiling. "Oh, this is my friend Seth and his
dad, Mr. Stevens, from Nebulon."

"Nice to meet you," said Grams.

"Thank you for letting us stay with
you," Mr. Stevens replied.

"Of course!" said Gramps. "Now, I heard a rumor that a fresh batch of Grams's famous peanut butter cookies are about to come out of the oven."

"What are we waiting for?!" cried Zack. The whole gang headed into the house.

Grams pressed a button on the wall next to her oven. The oven door slid open and a tray of steaming cookies appeared. Grams scooped up the cookies and put them on a plate.

"You bake the cookies yourself?" Seth asked, amazed. "Why do you not just have Ira do it for you?"

"Who's Ira?" asked Grams.

"It's our Indoor Robotic Assistant

back on Nebulon," Zack explained. "He's one of the many cool inventions we have there."

"Well, I don't think any robot could match Grams's peanut butter cook-ies," said Gramps.

Zack and Seth each grabbed a warm cookie and started munching.

"Oh, these are really good!" said
Seth. He snatched another cookie. "I
do not know if Ira could make cookies
this good!"

"So, I want to hear all about
Nebulon," said Grams.

"Me too!" said someone from the
doorway.

Chapter 5
Forkus Hagnus

"Bert!" shouted Zack. He ran over to greet his best friend on Earth. The two boys quickly completed their super-special handshake. First they gave each other high fives with their right hands. Then with their left hands. Finally they each lifted a fist into the air and bumped them together.

"And I wouldn't mind one of Gram's famous peanut butter cookies!" said Bert.

"Certainly, dear," said Grams.

"Bert, this is my friend Seth from Nebulon," said Zack. "Seth, this is Bert.

Bert remembered
how people said hi on
Nebulon. He lifted his
hand with his palm fac-
ing out. Then he moved
it in a small circle in front
of his face.

Seth did the same thing. He
was glad that he didn't have
to do the special Earth
handshake. It looked
hard.

Zack filled Grams,
Gramps, and Bert
in on his life on

Nebulon. He talked about his school, his friends, his house, the amazing inventions, the different foods, the vivi-vids, and anything else cool he could think of.

"So, Bert," he said when he was finished, "what parts of Dubbsville should we show Seth?"

"The atomic skateboard park, of course," said Bert. "And the mountain bike speedway."

"But what will we ride?" asked Seth. "My Torkus Magnus is back on Nebulon."

"Your Torkus who?" asked Gramps, scratching his head.

"The Torkus Magnus is the fastest bike on Nebulon," Zack explained.

"Well, I have a couple of bikes," said Gramps. "Let's take a look."

Gramps led the three boys to the garage. There he pulled out two dusty

old bikes. Lights flashed along the handlebars. A button in the middle of the handlebars was labeled FASTER. A square solar panel sat on the back bumper of each bike.

"These were pretty high-tech a few years back," Gramps said proudly.

"I cannot believe I have to ride some old Earth bike," said Seth.

"Well, it's not a Forkus Hagnus, but it'll get you there!" said Gramps.

Zack laughed. "It's Torkus Magnus, Gramps. Bert, why don't we all meet up after school tomorrow?" he suggested.

"Sounds good to me," said Bert. "See you guys then! Thanks for the cookies, Grams."

That night, Seth and his dad shared one of Grams and Gramps's guest rooms. Zack and his dad shared another. Zack was tired out from traveling and fell asleep quickly.

When he woke up the next morning, Zack hurried downstairs. Dad and Mr. Stevens had left for a business meeting.

"Good morning, Grams, Gramps," said Zack.

"How about some blueberry pancakes?" asked Gramps.

"That sounds delicious," said Zack. "Hey, where's Luna? She's probably hungry too."

"I let her out into the backyard a little while ago," said Grams.

Zack opened the door and stepped out into the back-yard. He looked all around. There was no sign of Luna.

Chapter 6

The Escape

Zack ran back into the house.

"Grams, Gramps!" he shouted. "I can't find Luna!"

Grams, Gramps, and Zack went out to the backyard. All the noise woke up Seth. He came downstairs and joined the others outside.

Seth looked around. "Do all Earth backyards have holes under their fences?" he asked. Seth pointed at a freshly dug hole at the bottom of the back fence.

"Luna dug her way out?" Zack cried. "But why would she do that?"

"More importantly," said Grams. "Where did she go?"

"Wait!" cried Zack. "Luna's wearing her geo-locator collar. I can track her on my hyperphone!"

"Geo-what?" asked Gramps. He scratched his chin. "Hyper-who?"

"It works like a tracking system," explained Zack. He already had his hyperphone out. "The locator satellite sends Luna's position right to the screen of my— found her!"

A small red dot flashed across a map on the screen of Zack's hyperphone.

"I don't believe it!" he cried. "I know exactly where Luna is headed. She's on her way to our old house! Come on, Seth. Let's go and get Luna!"

Zack and Seth jumped onto the bicycles Gramps had pulled out for them. Grams handed Zack his back-pack. Gramps handed them each helmets.

Zack pedaled hard, leading the way toward the place he used to live.

Seth hadn't ridden a bike with pedals since he was little. He was nervous.

"Where is my Torkus Magnus when I need it?" Seth whined. He concentrated hard on keeping his feet on the pedals. By the time they got down the street, Seth had gotten the hang of it. His feet remembered what to do!

The boys rode past a playground.

"Hey, what is that?" Seth asked. He pointed to a spinning ride in the park.

"That's the jet-powered carousel," Zack explained. "I used to ride that all the time when I lived here. Those little

rockets are powered by anti-grav jet units. It speeds around and around. Pretty grape, huh?"

"I do not know," replied Seth. "Even as a little kid, I think I would have rather watched a vivi-vid."

Zack shrugged and kept on pedaling.

"Speaking of speed," said Zack. "Press the faster button on your bike."

Zack and Seth both pressed the faster buttons on their bikes. The bikes'

solar panels flapped open. The extra power sent the bikes zooming along at twice the speed they had been going.

"This is more like it!" cried Seth.

As Zack rode along the familiar streets, he began to feel a little sad. He thought about his old life on Earth.

"Maybe Luna ran away because she doesn't like living on Nebulon,"

Zack said. He sounded worried. "Maybe she was happier here."

"Do not be silly, Zack," said Seth. "How could anyone, even a dog, think that Earth is better? Nebulon is *way* more grape."

Even if it wasn't true, Zack wanted to believe that Luna liked Nebulon.

Chapter 7
The Old
House

The boys arrived at Zack's old house. Zack knocked on the front door. It felt very strange not to burst in like he always used to.

A short woman opened the door. She had green skin and three eyes in her large head. Zack recognized her as a Kalosian.

"May I help you?" the woman asked. All three of her eyes blinked at the same time.

"Sorry to bother you. I'm Zack Nelson. I used to live in this house. I'm visiting Earth and my dog ran away. I think she might be here. She is brown and white and about this tall. Have you seen her?"

"Why, yes, actually" the woman said. She blinked again. "A dog ran into the backyard a while ago. But—"

"Thanks a lot!" said Zack. And before the woman could finish, he and Seth ran around the side of the house to the backyard. It looked pretty much the same as it did when he lived there.

"Luna's doghouse!" Zack cried. He pointed to a small metal doghouse sitting in the backyard. "My dad and I built it together when Luna was a puppy."

"What is that satellite dish for?" asked Seth.

"It tracks the weather outside. Then it changes the temperature inside the doghouse so that it is always comfortable," Zack explained.

Zack wondered why he had never thought about making a doghouse for Luna on Nebulon. He had assumed she preferred sleeping on his bed. Maybe he had been wrong.

Zack heard something move inside the doghouse.

"Luna!" he cried. He hurried over. "Is that you, girl?"

A huge head popped out of the doghouse.

This wasn't Luna. In fact, it wasn't even a dog.

A creature stepped out of the doghouse. It had six short stubby legs. Rough purple scales ran along its

back. Three fangs stuck out from its wide jaw.

Zack and Seth took a few steps back.

"Oh no," said Zack. "Did this thing eat Luna?"

Chapter 8
Chasing Luna

The Kalosian woman stepped up behind Zack. "Of course not," she said.

The fierce-looking creature whimpered and crawled back into the doghouse.

"Pookie is a Kalosian farg," the

woman explained. "They make the sweetest pets, but they are afraid of everything. In fact, your dog nearly scared the scales off of poor Pookie. I was trying to tell you that she dug up my flowers. I tried to lead her out of the backyard by her collar, but she wriggled free. The collar came off and she ran away."

The woman handed Luna's collar to
Zack. He stuffed it into his backpack.

"I'm really sorry Luna ruined your
flowers," said Zack. "And I'm sorry
she scared Pookie."

Zack and Seth headed back to
their bikes.

"How are we going to find her with-
out the geo-locator collar?" Seth asked.

"I don't know," said Zack.

The boys pedaled out into the street
just as the mail truck drove by. As it
passed each house, the truck fired a
bundle of mail from its laser-guided

letter launcher. Each bundle landed perfectly in the correct mailbox.

"Luna used to chase that truck all the time." said Zack. "She thought the mailman wanted to play catch with her."

Did I play catch with Luna enough on Nebulon? Zack wondered for a moment. Then he forced himself to focus.

"Maybe the mailman saw Luna!" he said. "He goes all over this neighborhood. Follow that truck!"

Seth and Zack sped off on their bikes.

"Mr. Geary!" Zack shouted.

The mail truck slowed to a stop. The boys quickly caught up.

"Well, if it isn't Zack Nelson!" said the mailman. "Haven't seen you since you moved."

"Yeah, we're visiting for a few days," Zack said quickly. "Have you seen—"

"Ya know, this is the second time today I've stopped," Mr. Geary said. "A dog tried to snatch the mail right out of the air. Looked a lot like your pesky dog, actually."

"Luna!" cried Zack. "Did you see which way she went?"

"Yup, she headed that way, toward the school," said Mr. Geary.

"The park!" Zack said. "She always loved the park behind the school. Thanks, Mr. Geary. Come on, Seth."

The boys raced to the park. Zack skidded to a stop. He jumped off his bike and stared at the park's soccer field. The field was covered with newly dug holes.

"Looks like Luna has been here," said Seth.

"Yes, but what in the galaxy is she looking for?" asked Zack.

"Zack!" shouted a voice from across the field.

"Bert!" Zack called back, spotting his best friend.

Bert sprinted across the field. "I was out-side for my lunch break and saw you guys."

"Bert, Luna's missing.

She ran away. We're trying to find her," Zack explained.

"Oh no!" said Bert. "Let me think. Have you tried the Dubbsville Pet Shop? She loved going there. Maybe she went to look for some bones to chew."

"Speaking of chewing, I am starving," said Seth. "Can we get some crispy fritters or a galactic patty around here?"

A bell sounded from the school.

"I have to go back to class. I'll meet you guys after school to help you look some more," said Bert. "Don't worry, Zack. We'll find her!" He turned and ran back across the field. "Good luck!" he shouted over his shoulder.

Zack turned to Seth. "There aren't any galactic patties, but we can grab some Biggie Burgers and Fantasti-Fries at Burger Universe," he said.

"Fine," said Seth. "Is it far?"

"No. Follow me," said Zack. He jumped onto his bike. "We'll grab a burger, then head to the pet store. We've got to find Luna today!"

Chapter 9

Spotted!

Zack and Seth hurried to Burger Universe.

"Where are the auto-ordering robots?" asked Seth. He and Zack grabbed a table.

"They don't have those on Earth," Zack explained. "You type your order

into this computer. It gets z-mailed to the kitchen. Then a tray with your food pops out of your table."

Zack typed an order for two Super Biggie Burgers, drinks, and a large order of Fantasti-Fries. Less than five minutes later, a tray with the food rose up from the boys' table. They began munching down their lunch.

"That was not bad," Seth admitted, when the boys finished. They hurried outside and got back onto their bikes.

Zack and Seth sped through the streets of Dubbsville. They passed a baseball field where a game was being played.

"What are they doing?" asked Seth. He slowed down his bike to watch.

"They're playing baseball," Zack explained. "It's just like galactic blast, only people go onto the field and play instead of robots. It's fun!"

"It is weird," said Seth.

The boys rode on.

"There's the pet shop!" Zack said, pointing ahead.

Their bikes squealed to a stop. Zack and Seth jumped off their bikes and hurried into the store. Zack looked around. No sign of Luna. He spotted a shelf full of dog bones. He grabbed one and stood there staring at it.

"What is the matter?" asked Seth.

"Luna loved these bones even as a puppy," said Zack softly. "I remember buying her first bone here. It was purple and squeaked when you squeezed it. She loved it."

Seth looked around curiously.

"This is where we got Luna, you know," Zack continued. "She came running across this floor and jumped right up into my arms. That's when I knew she was my dog."

walked over to Zack and dropped the bone at his feet. It squeaked when it hit the sidewalk.

Zack knelt down and picked up the bone. His eyes opened wide. Zack started laughing. Luna licked his face.

"What is it, Zack?" asked Bert.

Zack held up the purple bone for his friends to see.

"This is the first bone I ever gave Luna," Zack explained. "She must have buried it when she was living with you, Bert. I forgot all about it when we moved. But Luna didn't forget, did you, girl?"

Zack scratched Luna's head. She wagged her tail and licked Zack's face again.

"She's been searching all of her old favorite places," said Zack. "She's

been trying to find her special bone the whole time!"

"So, she just wanted to bring it home to Nebulon," said Bert.

"*Home to Nebulon,*" thought Zack.

That sounds good. I guess Nebulon really has become my home. And Luna's home too.

Zack turned to Seth. "I'm sorry I couldn't really show you around like I planned," he said.

"Are you kidding?" Seth replied. "I saw lots of grape Earth stuff. The jet-powered carousel kind of looked like fun. So did the baseball game. I liked seeing your old house. And I have to admit that Earth food is not so bad. That Biggie Burger was almost as good as a galactic patty!"

"All right, then," said Zack, smiling. "Who's ready to go to the mountain bike speedway? I think we have enough time before our shuttle leaves for home."

"You bet, Zack," said Bert. "That would be *grape*."

Zack smiled as Bert got his bike, and the three boys rode off. Luna trotted happily beside them, carrying her favorite bone in her mouth.

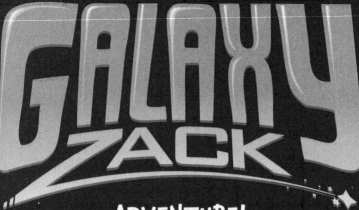

ADVENTURE!

HERE'S A SNEAK PEEK!

Zack Nelson unrolled his sleeping bag on the floor of his friend Drake's bedroom. Zack was at Drake's house for a sleepover. It was Friday night, and Halloween was just a week away!

Zack felt a bit sad. Halloween had been one of his favorite holidays on

An excerpt from *A Haunted Halloween*

Earth. Now Zack and his family lived on the planet Nebulon. On Nebulon, no one had even heard of Halloween!

"So you dress up in costumes?" asked Drake.

Zack had just finished telling him all about Halloween.

"Yup," said Zack.

"And you go from house to house, and people give you *free* candy?" Drake asked in disbelief.

"That's right," replied Zack. "And we tell ghost stories too."

"Ghost? What is a ghost?" asked Drake. "I have never heard of it."

An excerpt from *A Haunted Halloween*

"How about I tell you a ghost story?" Zack suggested. "I think that's the best way to explain what they are."

"Sure, I love stories," said Drake.

Drake curled up in his blanket. Zack turned down the light and pulled his sleeping bag over his head. He switched on a small astro-light and placed it under his chin. The glowing metal stick sent a weird shadow across his face.

Zack began his story.

An excerpt from *A Haunted Halloween*

ORYAN   FLT
O'Ryan, Ray.
Return to Earth! /

04/15